TRANSFORMERS

RISE OF THE BEASTS

The Search Is On

Adapted by Patty Michaels

Based on the screenplay written by
Joby Harold and Darnell Metayer & Josh Peters and Erich Hoeber & Jon Hoeber

Illustrated by Guido Guidi

Simon Spotlight
New York   London   Toronto   Sydney   New Delhi

SIMON SPOTLIGHT
An imprint of Simon & Schuster Children's Publishing Division
1230 Avenue of the Americas, New York, New York 10020
This Simon Spotlight edition May 2023
TRANSFORMERS and HASBRO and all related trademarks and logos are trademarks of Hasbro, Inc.
© 2023 Hasbro. © 2023 Paramount Pictures Corporation.
All rights reserved, including the right of reproduction in whole or in part in any form.
SIMON SPOTLIGHT and colophon are registered trademarks of Simon & Schuster, Inc.
For information about special discounts for bulk purchases, please contact Simon & Schuster
Special Sales at 1-866-506-1949 or business@simonandschuster.com.
Manufactured in the United States of America 0423 LAK
10 9 8 7 6 5 4 3 2 1
ISBN 978-1-6659-2253-1 (pbk)
ISBN 978-1-6659-2254-8 (ebook)

Optimus Prime and the rest of the Autobots were on an important mission. They had to capture the Transwarp Key.

"In the past this key was used to open space-time portals across the galaxy," Optimus Prime said. "If we recover this key, we can use it to reunite all the Autobots scattered among the stars. Then we can open a Transwarp gate to Cybertron and save our people."

But after a battle between the Autobots and the Terrorcons, the Autobots had been defeated. Scourge and his army of Terrorcons had successfully stolen half of the Transwarp Key! Without the key, the future of the Autobots was in danger and so were their lives!

That is, until a robot named Airazor flew toward them to save them. "I am a Maximal. A warrior from both your past . . . and future," she told Optimus Prime, the Autobots, and their friends Elena and Noah. She also told them that while Scourge had half of the key, the other half was still missing. Could Airazor help Optimus Prime and the Autobots find the missing half?

Elena worked in a museum and knew a lot about old artifacts and archaeology. She peered at her notebook. "It's in Peru," she told them. "The symbols on the stone . . . they've only been recorded in one other place in th world. The Inca Temple of the Sun, in Cusco. It's one of the oldest buildings the Western Hemisphere."

"We must go and find it before Scourge does," Optimus Prime said. He summoned the Autobot Stratosphere to take them to Peru in his plane mode.

When they arrived, Airazor soared overhead to help search for the missing half of the key. She spotted a church below her and detected traces of Energon. Energon was fuel used by the Transformers bots that could take any form—liquid, crystal, raw energy, or gas. Could the missing half of the key be close by?

The city below Airazor was packed with people celebrating a festival in the town. Mirage gave Noah a gauntlet and wondered if the Transformers robots should wait until the festival was over so the people wouldn't get hurt.

"No," Optimus Prime said. "If we could track the key here, so could Scourge. We must go now and retrieve it before he does."

Meanwhile Scourge and the Terrorcons were perched on a highway above the festival, looking down at the crowd. Nightbird spotted Noah and Elena. "The Autobots are using them to reach the temple," he said. "Good," Scourge replied. "We'll let them do the work for us."

At the same time, Noah and Elena had just arrived in a large courtyard. "The key has got to be here somewhere," Noah said, looking around. Just then Elena spotted what appeared to be a large sundial amid the stones.

Elena and Noah cleared weeds from the stones, exposing what was indeed a sundial. Elena read the strange script that was carved into the stone. Then she noticed a familiar-looking symbol.

"That's the symbol on Airazor's chest," she realized. "But it's not lined up right." She grabbed one of the rings around the symbol and pulled it. Noah helped her. The symbol parts were now lined up, revealing the crest of . . . the Maximals! At that moment, they heard a loud rumble and the center of the sundial fell away, revealing a spiral staircase.

Noah and Elena began to carefully descend the staircase. When they reached the bottom, they looked around in awe.

"We're probably the first people to walk here in thousands of years," Elena said.

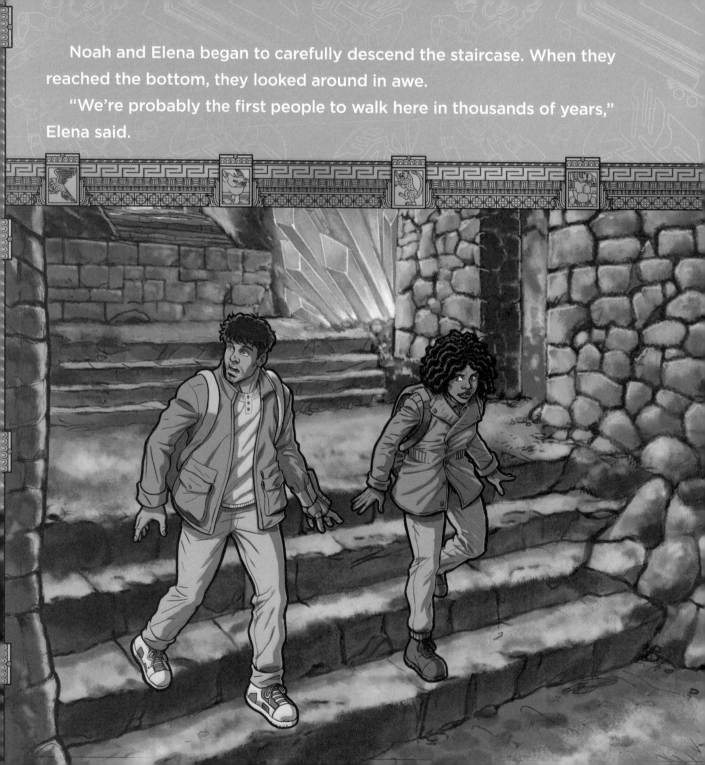

Suddenly she spotted [a] stone tabernacle. Maybe [th]e key was inside! They [str]uggled to lift the lid off [th]e tabernacle. But it was [em]pty. The Transwarp Key [w]as not there.

They heard a loud sound. It was Freezer, one of the Terrorcons! Noah and Elena [al]erted the Autobots that they were being chased.

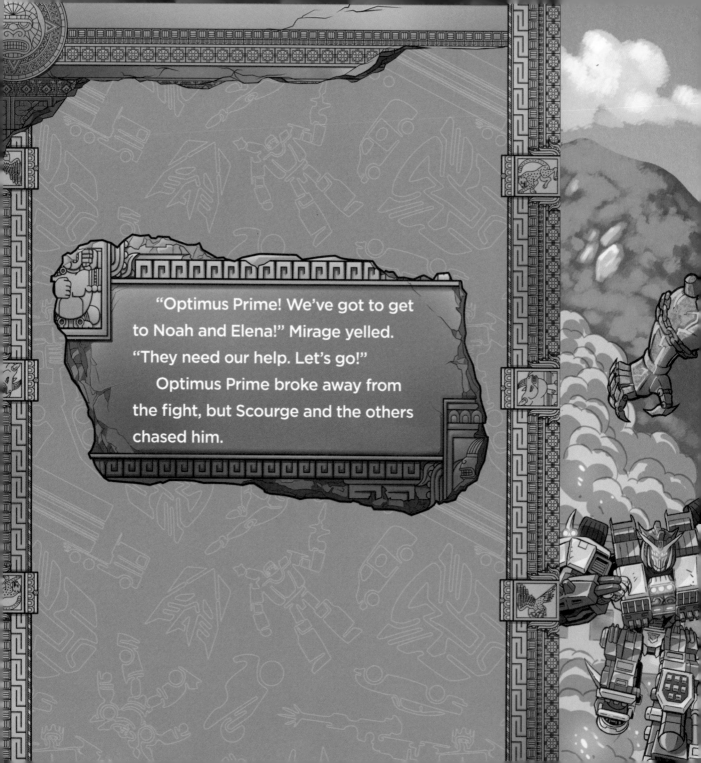

"Optimus Prime! We've got to get to Noah and Elena!" Mirage yelled. "They need our help. Let's go!"

Optimus Prime broke away from the fight, but Scourge and the others chased him.

Elena and Noah raced through the cave to escape. Just then they spotted a huge creature with sharp fangs, long claws, and glowing yellow eyes. The creature let out a loud ROAR. It was Cheetor!

"Run!" Noah shouted.

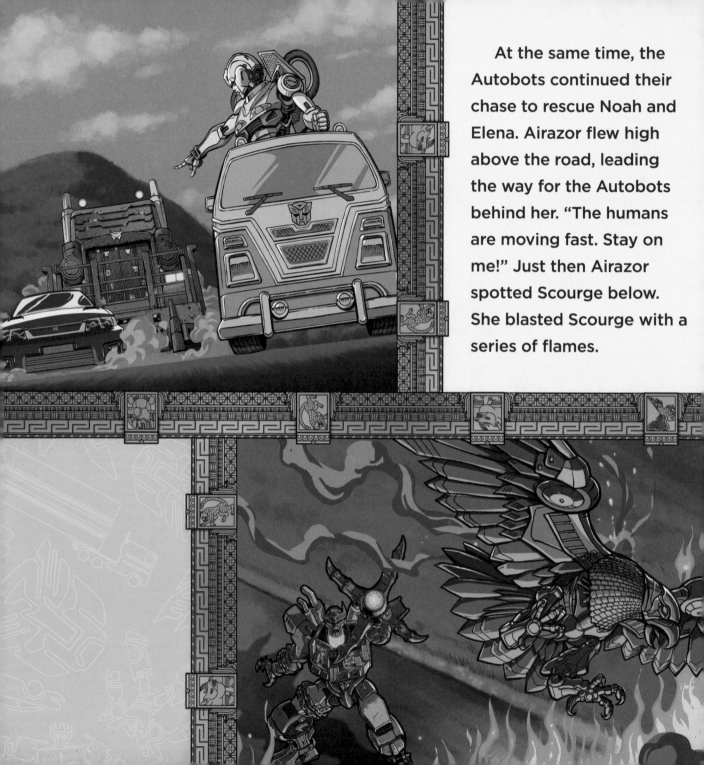

At the same time, the Autobots continued their chase to rescue Noah and Elena. Airazor flew high above the road, leading the way for the Autobots behind her. "The humans are moving fast. Stay on me!" Just then Airazor spotted Scourge below. She blasted Scourge with a series of flames.

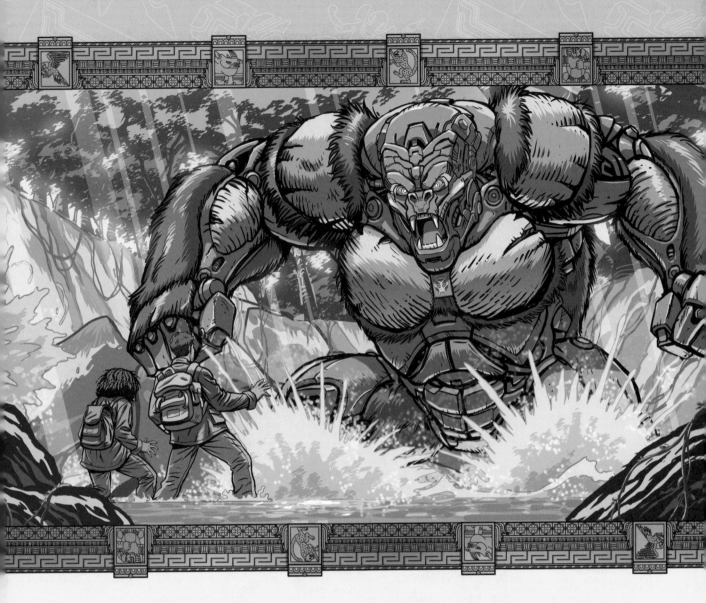

Elena and Noah managed to escape Cheetor and safely exit the cave. They landed in a shallow pool of water in the jungle. But they weren't safe just yet. In front of them was a gigantic metallic gorilla with blazing blue eyes. It was Primal. "Who are you?" Primal roared. "Why are you hunting for the key?"

Noah and Elena raced away from Primal. Luckily, Optimus Prime and the Autobots had arrived to help.

"Let them go. NOW!" Optimus Prime ordered, as Cheetor and Mirage scuffled.

Just then Airazor revealed a stunning secret. "These are my fellow Maximals," she said. "Cheetor, Rhinox, and our leader, Optimus Primal," Airazor continued. "Scourge has come to Earth, and he has half of the key," she explained to the Maximals. "We must find the second piece before he does."

"We moved the key long ago to keep it safe," Primal revealed to Airazor and the Autobots. "Why do you want it?" he asked Optimus Prime.

"If I don't get back to my planet soon, I will lose my people," Optimus Prime said.

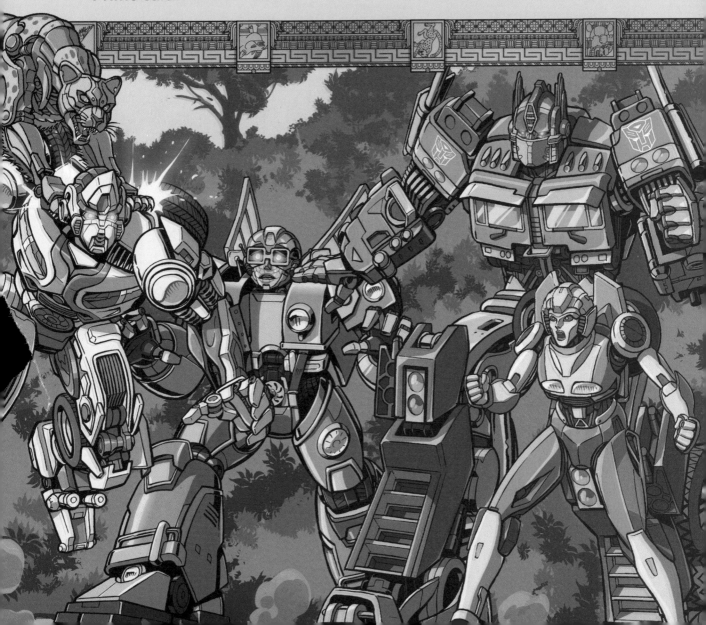

"Come with me," Primal told Optimus Prime and the Autobots. Primal led them to a small house in the village. A little girl appeared carrying a wooden box. She opened the lid of the box, revealing the other half of the key! Primal had put his trust in humans to keep it safe.

"It will be night soon," Primal said. "Tomorrow we will light the key's beacon and bring Scourge to us."

Optimus Prime was thrilled that the other half of the key had been discovered. But now it was time for the battle of their lives against Scourge and the Terrorcons.